1/18

The
Wishing
Tree

Written by **Mary Redman**

Illustrated by **Christina Rodriguez**

Elva Resa ✳ Saint Paul

The Wishing Tree
Text © 2008 Mary Redman
Illustrations © 2008 Christina Rodriguez

Design by Andermax Studios.

Library of Congress Cataloging-in-Publication Data

Redman, Mary, 1962-
   The wishing tree / written by Mary Redman; illustrated by Christina Rodriguez.
      p. cm.
   Summary: When her father leaves for a deployment, to try to make the waiting
easier for herself, Amanda decides to make a wishing tree. Includes instructions
and information about wishing trees.
   ISBN 978-1-934617-02-1 (hardcover)
   [1. Children of military personnel — Fiction. 2. Wishes — Fiction.]
   I. Rodriguez, Christina, ill. II. Title.
   PZ7.R24489Wi 2008
   [E] — dc22

2008026433

Printed in Canada.
1 2 3 4 5 6 7 8 9 10

Elva Resa Publishing
Saint Paul, Minnesota
http://www.elvaresa.com

For military families everywhere,
with much gratitude and appreciation — MR

For my sister, Angela,
with special thanks to the Nazaroffs — CER

Amanda scanned the line of troops for her father's face. She waved one more time, hoping he could see her.

"How long is Dad going to be gone?" Amanda asked her mother again.

"At least a year," her mother said.

Amanda's words were a whisper. "I'm really going to miss him."

Amanda and her mother watched as the plane tore down the runway and lifted into the sky. *The world has changed and my dad is going to help make it better*, Amanda reminded herself.

"Mom, I'm worried about Dad."

"I'm worried too. Let's come up with something to make this deployment a little easier," her mother suggested.

"Like what?" Amanda couldn't think of a thing.

"Oh, I don't know, how about ice cream sundaes for dinner every Sunday?" her mother teased. Amanda smiled, but she didn't think ice cream once a week would be enough.

Amanda rolled ideas around in her mind on the ride home. She could write her thoughts in a journal. Or she could take pictures and make an album of her year. She spotted a tree with yellow ribbons tied to the branches.

"That's it!" she said, "A wishing tree!"

"Mom, I'll make a wishing tree, and I'll write my wishes, hopes, and prayers on a piece of ribbon every day Dad's gone," Amanda said. "And I'll make them yellow, like the ribbons you see in support of the troops."

"What a great idea," her mother said with a smile.

They stopped at a craft store. Amanda chose a small artificial tree, some bright yellow ribbon, and a pen.

She removed all the silk leaves from the little tree. It looked forlorn and bare.

Amanda grabbed her scissors and cut a strip
of ribbon. *I hope your flight is safe* she wrote. She tied
the ribbon to a branch on the tree. With even one
new yellow leaf, it looked a little less bleak.

The next day she wrote her father a long letter. Then
she wrote another wish. *Please protect my daddy from harm.*
With a second ribbon, the tree looked almost cheerful.

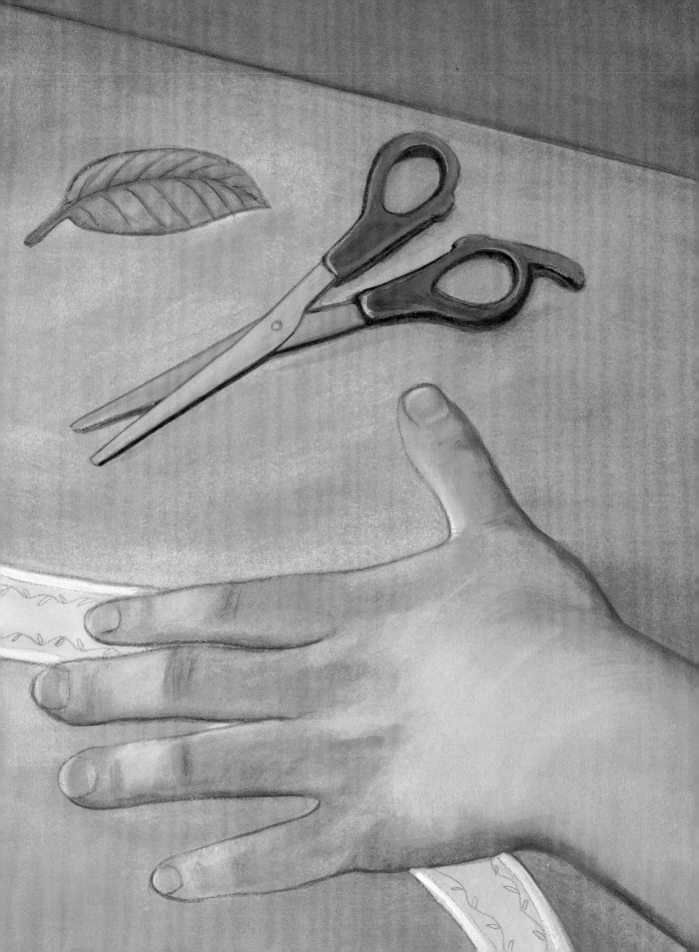

Every day she wrote a wish for her dad. Sometimes it was for his safety, and sometimes it was for him to send her an e-mail.

Sometimes the e-mail didn't come.

"Mom, I wished for an e-mail, but Dad hasn't sent me one in over a week!" Amanda said.

"We don't always get what we wish for," her mother said. "And there are times we have to wait longer than we would like. You know your dad would send one if he could. Think about all the things he has done."

Amanda looked through the pictures,
cards, e-mails, and letters her father had sent since he left.
She wrote *I love you Dad* on the day's ribbon and tied it
to the top of the highest branch on the tree.

Each day Amanda faithfully wrote another ribbon.

She wished her father good meals and clean sheets. Yellow ribbons blossomed like daffodils on the empty branches.

She wished him nice friends and good luck. And the wishing tree bloomed brighter.

She wished he would come home soon.

The tree grew lush with yellow leaves. It glowed like a radiant little oak in autumn.

"Mom!" Amanda called out one day near the end of her dad's deployment. "I can't find a place to tie a ribbon."

Her mother leaned in the doorway with a smile on her face and the phone in her hand. "You only need room for two more. I just got word that Dad is coming home."

Amanda wrote the ribbons out right away and tied them around the trunk. *Thank you! Thank you!*

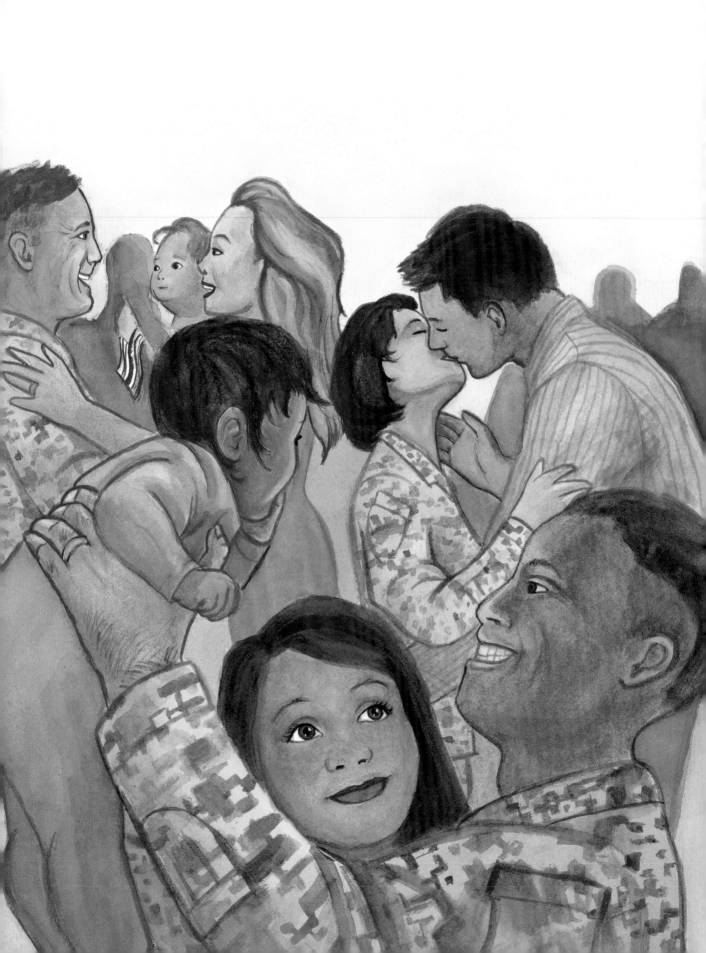

There was a huge celebration for the homecoming. All the families dressed up and arrived hours early. They waved flags and smiled until their mouths hurt.

Amanda held her father's large, warm hand on the ride home.

When he walked into the house, the first thing her father saw was the wishing tree. He gave Amanda a puzzled look.

Amanda beamed. He had noticed her tree bursting with bright yellow fabric. "It's my wishing tree, Dad. Every day you were gone I added one wish to the branches. It made me feel like I was helping you."

Her dad untied and read every wish right then and there. Some made him laugh. Some brought tears to his eyes. All the wishes let him know how much his daughter loved him.

He turned to Amanda and hugged her tight.
"You did help me, Princess, you did."

About Wishing Trees

Wishing trees exist in many cultures around the world. For more than 100 years, the Chinese have been tossing wishes written on red and gold paper attached to oranges into the Lam Tsuen wishing trees in Hong Kong. In England, there's an old Hawthorn tree near a castle with pennies pushed into the bark like coins thrown into a fountain. In India, Turkey, and Japan, people write wishes on bits of white paper and tie them to trees. Charities in many western countries decorate holiday trees with gift requests. There are even web sites with virtual wishing trees.

With a little imagination, you can make your own wishing tree. Use a small artificial tree like Amanda's, an indoor plant, or a pine or other holiday tree. It can be as simple as a tree branch in a block of florist's foam (available at craft stores). Pick out some ribbon and a fabric pen and wish away.

Mary Redman has experienced many joys and challenges as a military wife and mother over the past 20 years. She has managed pack-outs, given birth, visited emergency rooms, heralded holidays, bid farewell to grandparents, and attended numerous school events while her husband was deployed. Military life gave Mary many unexpected opportunities, from attending the running of the bulls in Spain to teaching English in Japan and exploring American history with her family in Virginia. She lives on Long Island with her husband and three boys, where she spends much of her time attending soccer games.

Born overseas to multicultural parents, **Christina Rodriguez** grew up as an "Air Force brat," moving from place to place. Christina loved to draw and paint. She was awarded a generous scholarship to the Rhode Island School of Design where she earned a fine arts degree in illustration. Christina is an award-winning children's book illustrator and in her spare time enjoys cooking authentic Mexican cuisine, volunteering, hula-hooping, and being outdoors. She and her husband live with their dog in historic Stillwater, Minnesota.